A BOY NAMED

ISAMU

A Story of ISAMU NOGUCHI

JAMES
YANG

VIKING

If you are a boy
named Isamu . . .

at the market with your mother,
it can be a crowded and noisy place.

Maybe there is a quiet space
that feels more like you.

Children are playing loudly.
You keep walking.

When it is quiet, you wonder . . . .

What kind of wood is this?

How does fruit get its color?

Why does cloth feel soft?

Who made the path with stone?

Paper lanterns are like another world far away from home.

How can light feel so welcoming?

In the forest, the trees tower over you as you hear the crunch of twigs under your feet.

The leaves are so perfect they
must have been waiting for you.

You toss grass in the air and watch
as blades scatter in different directions.

When you close your eyes,
you imagine the grass comes
back to you.

If you are Isamu, stones are the most special of all.
Time has carved each stone to be different.

How can they be so heavy?
Would they float if they had no weight?

They can be smooth or rough.

You press your ear against the stone.
What is it saying?

At the beach,
your stick makes a *shhhhhh* in the sand.

The ocean greets you
with its quiet rumble.

You feel like
the only person
in the world.

If you are Isamu, you find a secret place
so you can look at the ocean and see
the shapes of things.

You see birds that look like stones . . .

and stones that
look like birds.

Bamboo can be many things, but you know it's meant to be played like a flute.

"Isamu!
There you are!"

Your mother asks about your day.
You think about how you were
alone but not lonely.

You take one more look at the sticks, pebbles, shells, and bamboo who were waiting for you.

The forest and beach were like friends giving you a gift.

If you are Isamu, you wish
every day could be this big.

Portrait of Isamu Noguchi as a child in Japan, 1909.

Isamu Noguchi with Energy Void, 1971.

AUTHOR'S NOTE

ISAMU NOGUCHI was a famous Japanese American artist born in Los Angeles in 1904 who made sculptures of paper, wood, and stone, as well as creating landscape design. He was interested in the essence of nature and that influenced his artwork. Noguchi also believed a child's way of experiencing the world was an important part of being an artist. He once said, "When an artist stopped being a child, he would stop being an artist."

Noguchi's father was Japanese and his mother was American. He moved with his mother to Tokyo when he was three. American children saw Noguchi as Japanese and Japanese children saw him as American. Noguchi was happy spending time by himself and exploring nature.

Noguchi has always been a hero of mine. I love how his shapes make stone and wood feel alive. Like Noguchi, I would spend time alone in nature as a child. I would bike to my favorite lake and sit for hours thinking about the bigger world. This story is how I imagine Isamu Noguchi explored nature, because as some children know, alone time can be the most special time of all.

James Yang

TO ALL THE TEACHERS WHO CONVINCED
MY PARENTS THAT AN ARTIST'S LIFE WAS POSSIBLE.

VIKING

An imprint of Penguin Random House LLC, New York

First published in the United States of America by Viking,

an imprint of Penguin Random House LLC, 2021

Visit us online at penguinrandomhouse.com.

LIBRARY OF CONGRESS CATALOGING-IN-PUBLICATION DATA IS AVAILABLE

Manufactured in China

ISBN 9780593203446

1   3   5   7   9   10   8   6   4   2

Book design by James Yang and Jim Hoover   Typeset in Le Havre Rough Centerline and Abadi MT Std

The illustrations in this book were created digitally with copious amounts of chicken wings, baked goods, and coffee.

This is a work of historical fiction. Apart from the well-known actual people, events, and locales that figure in the narrative,

all names, characters, places, and incidents are the products of the author's imagination or are used fictitiously.

Any resemblance to current events or locales, or to living persons, is entirely coincidental.

The publisher does not have any control over and does not assume any responsibility for author or third-party websites or their content.

T 128154